bindi
Wildlife Adventures

BOOK 2

RESCUE!

Bindi Irwin

with Jess Black

sourcebooks
jabberwocky

Copyright © Random House Australia 2010
Cover photograph © Australia Zoo
Cover and internal design by Christabella Designs
Cover and internal design © 2011 by Sourcebooks, Inc.
Sourcebooks and the colophon are registered trademarks of Sourcebooks, Inc.

Published by Sourcebooks Jabberwocky, an imprint of Sourcebooks, Inc.
P.O. Box 4410, Naperville, Illinois 60567-4410
(630) 961-3900
Fax: (630) 961-2168
www.jabberwockykids.com

First published by Random House Australia in 2010.

Library of Congress Cataloging-in-Publication data is on file with the publisher.

Source of Production: Versa Press, East Peoria, Illinois, USA
Date of Production: February 2011
Run Number: 14566

Printed and bound in the United States of America.
VP 10 9 8 7 6 5 4 3 2 1

Dear Diary,

I've just come back from Africa. WOW!
What a place! I went on this amazing
horse trek with Hannah, one of my best
friends. She lives on a farm near the
town of Musina in Limpopo Province,
which is in the northeastern corner
of South Africa.

 We were meant to be riding so we
could see the amazing African wildlife
but we got a little sidetracked. And if
we hadn't got sidetracked, we never
would have found out about the
endangered sable antelope and
the game hunters or got
caught trying to help. And,
believe it or not, that's
only half the story!

Bindi

CHAPTER ONE

From the window in Hannah's bedroom, Bindi watched in awe as dawn broke over a beautiful view of the African bush. Right out the front of the farmhouse was a giant baobab tree that Bindi was itching to climb. It had a really wide, gnarly trunk, which was so different from the skinny gum trees back home. She felt sure that from the top of that tree you would be able to see the whole country.

But climbing it would have to wait, because the trekkers had an early start. Hannah's mum, Kirsten, ran a horse-trekking business called Trailblazers in Limpopo, South Africa, for tourists who were keen to see African wildlife. Limpopo was filled with game parks and nature reserves. It was a really pretty corner of the country with a wide variety of native animals.

Bindi, her mum, Terri, and brother, Robert, had been staying in Cape Town to film a movie and had arrived the day before for a short visit before heading home to Australia. Bindi and Hannah would spend the next three days riding with Thabu, Trailblazers' most senior guide. Thabu and his family lived and worked at the farm. They were of the North Sotho tribe.

"Which horse is going to be mine?" cried Bindi excitedly as she raced out of the farmhouse toward the stables.

Hannah was already there, setting up for the ride. She laughed at Bindi's enthusiasm. "Mum told me I should let you sleep in."

"No way. How could I sleep in when I'm this excited?!" Bindi couldn't decide what she thought was going to be the best part of the ride: roughing it in the wild for three days, cooking their own food, or seeing every kind of African creature, from a dung beetle to an elephant!

Thabu smiled at Bindi's energy as he took her to meet her horse. He was a palomino, a tan horse with a beautiful white mane and tail.

"What's his name, Thabu?" she asked as she stroked the horse's neck and spoke gently to him. He seemed to like it. Bindi knew they were going to be very good friends.

"His name is Koto."

"Koto. Ko-to." Bindi loved to practice saying words in a different language. They didn't sound anything like Aussie words!

Hannah was busy saddling her own horse. She was a gray mare (which in horse language meant white) named Pippi. She was named after Pippi Longstocking, because she had black markings on her legs that looked just like stockings. Bindi couldn't wait to see Hannah ride; she knew she was really good.

Terri and Kirsten came outside

carrying the food and water the riders would need for the trek. "I think you'll really like the food Kirsten's prepared for you," called Terri. As Terri knew, Bindi always got really hungry when they went camping. Food was something she looked forward to.

While Terri packed the saddle bags, Kirsten turned to Bindi and Hannah with a serious expression. "Now remember, girls, you'll be seeing lots of wild animals in their own habitat. You are to obey Thabu at all times. You might be riding in a game park but this is *no game!* Okay?"

She waited for both girls to nod their understanding before she went on.

"When you're riding the horses, their sweat and scent overpowers your own human smell. This means you're able to get closer to the wildlife without them realizing. It's a different story when you're on foot. At the campsite you must stay close to Thabu. No wandering off."

The girls nodded again, this time a little distractedly. They couldn't wait to get going!

Kirsten smiled. "Well, have fun!"

Bindi gave Terri a quick good-bye hug. She looked around for Robert.

He had made friends with Thabu's son, Mpho. The boys were the same age and had bonded over Mpho's promise to show Robert every lizard hideout on the property. Bindi noticed the two of them huddled over something in the dirt.

Bindi called out to Robert as she mounted Koto. "See you later, alligator!"

"Wait up! I've got a present for you, Bindi!" Robert ran up to her, carrying something wrapped in cloth. He slipped the gift into Bindi's saddle bag. "But you can't open it until later."

"Thanks!" Bindi was too excited

about the ride to pay the surprise gift much attention. "See you all soon!"

"Bye, Bindi! Bye, Hannah! See you, Thabu!"

The remaining group stood around the stable yard waving. Robert and Mpho dashed away almost immediately—they had lizards to find. Terri was going to be kept busy helping Kirsten with some repair work around the farm.

The three horses and their riders headed out of the stables and slowly made their way into the grassland.

Away from the farmlands, they were soon deep in the heart of the bush, surrounded by thorn trees and baobabs. The horses' ears pricked back and forth, listening to the sound of birds and the distant calls of wildlife.

Bindi felt a rush of excitement. The earth felt alive and she was very much a part of it.

CHAPTER TWO

It didn't matter how many countries Bindi visited, she never lost her sense of wonder about being somewhere completely new.

Here she was in Africa! The air smelled different. The water tasted different. Even the ground was different. In this part of Africa the soil was a rich red color. It was as if someone had spilled a pot of red paint and it had seeped deep into the earth.

They rode in single file with Thabu in the lead and Hannah bringing up the back. Bindi liked being in the middle—that way she could talk to both Hannah and Thabu.

So far that morning they had heard the calls of lots of animals but not actually seen any. They had even played a guessing game where you had to try to name the animal by its call. Thabu was the judge, as he was an expert when it came to African animals.

Thabu held up his hand, signaling for them to stop. They had communicated a few times that morning using hand signals. Hannah had explained that the sounds of their voices could scare off any nearby animals.

They waited, wondering what could be lurking nearby. Then, to Bindi's disappointment, Thabu signaled for them to keep riding. Another false alarm! Bindi was beginning to wonder if there really *were* any wild animals living in Africa.

"When will we see a lion, Thabu?"

Bindi asked. Bindi loved lions. She especially liked their cute cubs.

"Who can say, Bindi?" was all Thabu answered.

They rode on for a little longer but the day was growing hot and it was time to rest the horses. They tied them up in the shade while they ate their lunch in a nearby hide.

A hide was a man-made shelter that blended into the bush. It allowed you to watch animals without them seeing you. This hide was next to a water hole. If they kept quiet they would be able to see the animals up close when they came for a drink.

The three of them sat in silence,

eating their sandwiches and watching the water hole. Still no animals. Bindi cleared her throat to speak. Thabu gave her a warning look and put his fingers to his lips. "Ah-ah."

Bindi sighed and whispered, "I just wondered when you think we'll see something."

Thabu smiled at her persistence. "The animals will come when you least expect it."

Hannah pressed a couple of animal-shaped biscuits into Bindi's hand. "In the meantime you can make do with these," she whispered with a quiet giggle.

Bindi stared at the bright pink

icing on her rhino-shaped biscuit. She wondered if it was the closest she would come to a real African animal. She bit down hard on the rhino's leg.

"Shhh!" Hannah held her finger to her lips and pointed.

Approaching the water hole was a herd of springbok. They were a native African antelope, brown and white in color, and they could run super-fast. There were about eight adult springbok and three young ones. They were very elegant. As they reached the water, they spread their spindly legs and dropped their heads to drink.

Bindi was spellbound. Finally she was seeing the real Africa!

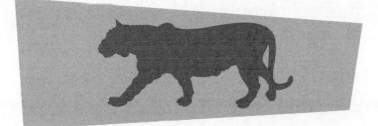

CHAPTER THREE

Bindi was glad when they finally approached their camping place for the night. She wasn't sure if she was going to be able to walk when she dismounted. Her legs felt very stiff but she didn't want to let on to Hannah and Thabu. They rode every day and probably wouldn't be sore at all.

Thabu called quietly to her and Hannah. "Looks like we have company." He pointed to a group of curious meerkats who were watching the three riders.

Bindi was thrilled. "They're sooooooo cute!"

The meerkats stood on their hind legs and seemed to be chattering about the strange humans they were looking at. They reminded Bindi of a group of kids gossiping. They had long slender bodies with big eyes and seemed to be constantly in a state of alertness.

"If we're quiet and make no sudden moves, they might stick around," said Thabu.

He dismounted slowly and the girls did the same.

Bindi grimaced as she tried to walk. Groaning loudly would have made her feel better about her stiff muscles, but she was determined to be as quiet as a mouse—she was not going to scare away those gorgeous meerkats.

Bindi reached into her saddle bags to unpack some of the cooking gear. Her hand brushed against the small package Robert had given her. She'd forgotten all about his surprise present. As the cloth wrapping came undone, an enormous hairy black spider sprung out from the material!

"Arggghhhh!" Bindi screamed into the quiet African dusk. The startled meerkats bounded off. A far-off flock of birds took flight from a tree they'd been nesting in. Hannah and Thabu rushed over to see what had happened. A scorpion bite? A snake attack?

"What's wrong?" cried Hannah.

Bindi pointed to the ground where she'd dropped the huge spider. It seemed to stare up at her. Typical. Everything else had been scared away by her scream but not the scary spider!

"A nasty little brother surprise is what's wrong!"

Thabu kneeled in the dirt and gently touched the spider with a stick. "It looks like a baboon spider." It didn't move. Thabu leaned in closer before picking up the creature with a smile.

"Arggghhhh!" cried the girls in unison as they backed away.

"A *fake* baboon spider." Thabu began to laugh. "It's made of rubber."

Bindi rolled her eyes. "You've got to be kidding me. My heart almost stopped beating!" When she saw

Hannah and Thabu give each other a quick smile, she felt a little foolish. What kind of wildlife warrior was scared of a rubber spider?

Once the horses were rubbed down and fed and the camp set up, three very hungry trekkers sat down to eat. The view was amazing and made even prettier by the pink haze of dusk. Thabu heated up their dinner. He explained that the slightly spicy mince dish was called bobotie and was a traditional South African meal. As Bindi gulped it down she thought it was the best food she'd ever tasted.

They could hear various animal sounds as night approached. They passed the time eating and listening to Hannah do her own imperson-ation of a few animal calls. She was really good!

Bindi noticed a tall wire fence to the west of the camp. "What's behind that fence?"

Thabu's face lit up. "We're very excited about this new sanctuary," he explained. "It's a new breeding center for the Angolan giant sable antelope. This breed of antelope is on the critically endangered list and needs to be protected."

"It's awesome that a sanctuary has been set up!" said Bindi. She loved hearing about animals being protected. "Maybe we can check it out?"

Thabu nodded. "I'd like to have a look myself. It's not out of our way. We can drop in tomorrow."

Hannah and Bindi were excited about the next day but were finding it hard to keep their eyes open. They packed up the dishes and brushed their teeth.

Bindi was about to crawl into the tent when she heard the

unmistakable growl of a lion close by.

She didn't panic at all. She tried to remember everything Thabu had taught her. She was to keep a clear head and not make any sudden moves. As her mind raced, her body remained still. A lion in the wild! Awesome! She had faith that Thabu would know what to do.

"Ahem."

Thabu was clearing his throat nearby. Bindi waited for him to give her instructions on how to stay safe.

"Hannah, that's enough for one night."

Huh?

The lion attempted to growl again but this time the sound dissolved into giggling. Bindi slowly turned to see Hannah behind her. She couldn't believe it—Hannah was the lion! That girl was seriously, seriously good at animal impersonations!

CHAPTER FOUR

Bindi was woken from a deep sleep by the sound of voices. At first she thought it was Thabu and Hannah and that it was time to get up. Then she realized it was dark outside and that Hannah was still fast asleep beside her.

Bindi listened but she couldn't understand what was being said. They were speaking in a different language.

"Hannah, wake up!" Bindi shook her friend.

Hannah groggily looked at her watch. "It's three o'clock in the morning!"

Bindi was wide awake. "There are people outside but I can't understand what they're saying."

Hannah listened. Bindi was right; Hannah could hear male voices and they were speaking in Afrikaans. "Something about sable and hunting, I think. It's hard to hear."

Bindi couldn't shake the feeling

that something was wrong. She started to get dressed.

"Come on. Let's follow them!"

Hannah knew Bindi well enough to know that it was pointless to argue with her once she'd made up her mind. The two girls hastily pulled on their boots, grabbed flashlights, and snuck out of their tent.

"What about Thabu?" whispered Hannah. "Should we wake him?"

Bindi shook her head. "We'll be back before he even notices we've gone."

Hannah was no tracker but as they could still hear the men talking, the girls followed the sound of their muffled voices. Luckily, the full moon gave just enough light to keep the night from being pitch black. After a little way, Bindi and Hannah found themselves following the metal fence they had seen the night before.

After several hundred feet the men stopped. They seemed to be having an argument. Bindi and Hannah crouched behind the trunk of a large thorn tree to watch.

Their eyes had now adjusted to the dim light. They could see two men dressed in khaki. It was impossible to really see what they looked like as they had smeared their faces with paint in browns and greens. They had gone to a lot of trouble to camouflage themselves.

The tallest man pulled a pair of wire cutters from his canvas bag and began to cut a hole in the fence.

Suddenly Bindi understood. These men wanted to break into the sanctuary. They'd mentioned hunting earlier. Maybe they were going to shoot or hurt one of the endangered antelopes. She'd heard about game parks selling animals to rich hunters for just this reason.

They had to be stopped!

Bindi leaned in close to Hannah and whispered in her ear. Hannah's eyes widened as she listened to her friend. Finally she nodded and gave Bindi the thumbs up.

The man cutting the fence motioned to his friend to help as he pulled back the tough steel fencing.

A loud and angry roar from a nearby lion rang out over the grasslands. The men froze in their tracks. The lion growled again. After a quick and heated debate, the men dropped their tools and sprinted back the way they had come.

Bindi and Hannah stepped out from behind their hiding place and high-fived each other.

"Way to go, Hannah! You sure

had them running scared." The girls couldn't stop giggling.

"Oh, I'm good!" Hannah was pleased as punch with her efforts! "Did you see how fast they ran?"

But Bindi was already investigating the equipment the men had left scattered on the ground.

Moments later, Bindi heard another loud growl from behind her.

"It's okay, Hannah!" said Bindi as she bent down to look at the wire cutters. "The men are long gone!"

"Ah, Bindi—" Hannah whispered quietly to her friend.

"Yeah, yeah, you're king of the jungle," joked Bindi, distracted.

"Turn around very slowly," Hannah cautioned. She pointed a little distance away from the wire fence. "Look."

Bindi turned to see what Hannah was pointing at.

Not ten feet from the girls, swishing a very angry tail, stood a fully grown lioness.

CHAPTER FIVE

Hannah and Bindi remained frozen to the spot. They watched transfixed as the lioness paced restlessly in front of them.

"Well, you got your lion," Hannah whispered to Bindi.

"Sure did," replied Bindi. It was just as Thabu had said. "Right when I least expected it."

The closer the lioness paced, the more she blocked off their only escape option. Hannah carefully backed up to where Bindi was pinned against the tall wire fence.

"Let's try moving slowly to the right," suggested Bindi. She took a step and indicated for Hannah to do the same.

But the lioness didn't like that and let out an angry growl. The girls froze.

Just then a gorgeous little lion cub came tumbling out of the bushes. The lioness nudged him with her nose while keeping a steady eye on the girls.

"No wonder she's upset," gasped Bindi. "She's got cubs to protect."

Bindi took another step. She knew that you should never get mixed up with a mother and her babies. The mother would do anything to protect them. They had to get away, and fast.

As Bindi took another step she stumbled on something sharp. She looked down to see the pair of wire cutters.

Of course!

She nudged Hannah. "Let's get to the hole in the fence!" It was their only hope—but the hole was closer to the lioness than they were!

Bindi took a deep breath. If they were very slow and still with their movements, the lioness might lose interest in them. She didn't seem to be on the lookout for food, which was a huge relief. The lioness kept a sharp eye on the girls as they began their slow journey toward the hole in the fence, keeping her cubs away from the two humans.

After what seemed like hours later, Bindi finally reached the break in the fence. She struggled to pull back the stiff and heavy steel mesh so that they could squeeze through.

"You go first, and make it quick!" Bindi nodded to Hannah while she held back the opening. With a swift glance at the lion, Hannah crawled through to the other side.

Bindi passed her the wire cutters and canvas bag the men had dropped. There might be food in the bag and it could be a long time before they found help.

Once Bindi was through to the other side, the girls looked for pieces of bush to cover up the hole. They didn't want a protective mother lion taking too much of an interest in them!

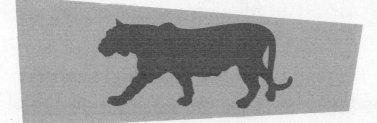

CHAPTER SIX

"Phew!" Hannah sank down to the ground as if her legs could no longer hold her. "Now *that* was scary."

Bindi joined her friend. "Yeah, definitely a close call!"

The sound of a distant engine

interrupted them, and they saw far-off headlights that were getting closer by the moment.

They jumped up for a better look and called out, "Hey, over here!" They did their best to get the driver's attention, Hannah waving the wire cutters.

A loudspeaker came on with a loud crackle. A voice rang out: "Drop your weapons and freeze!"

In an instant they were blinded by the jeep's headlights.

The girls instantly dropped the gear they were carrying. Weapons? What were they talking about?

"These aren't weapons!" cried

Bindi. "We took this stuff from the men who broke in through the fence."

The jeep screeched to a halt and two men approached the girls. It was difficult to see their faces through the glare of the high beams.

"Men? Seems to me it's just you two troublemakers carrying what look very much like wire cutters."

The man grabbed the canvas bag from Hannah and opened it. He whistled in disbelief and held up a camera with a very large lens. "And I'll be guessing that this is your camera?"

The girls shook their heads. "It's not ours," stuttered Hannah.

"I guess you won't miss it then." The man threw the camera down hard onto the ground. It smashed into tiny pieces.

"Yikes," whispered Hannah to Bindi. "Why would he do that? It's an expensive piece of equipment."

"No talking! You two can save your story for the police." The man motioned for the girls to follow him. "We take trespassing pretty seriously."

Bindi and Hannah realized they had no choice but to follow the men into the waiting jeep.

Bindi whispered to Hannah, "I have a bad feeling about this."

Hannah nodded and bent over to tie a shoelace. "I'd rather have taken my chances with the lioness," she muttered.

The girls were driven to the main office of the park and told to wait. The sanctuary manager had been called and was on his way to interview them. Bindi felt sure that when he heard what they had to say, this misunderstanding would quickly be cleared up.

In the meantime, all they could do was sit down and wait. Bindi saw Hannah stifle a yawn. A moment later Bindi was holding back a yawn of her own, and then Hannah started up again. Yawning was totally contagious and it was now about 4:30 a.m. They hadn't got quite as much sleep as they'd planned and the office wasn't very interesting. It was very bare apart from a large poster of a majestic giant sable antelope that dominated the room. Bindi had never seen one before and marveled at the power of the animal. It had beautiful shiny eyes, a muscular body, and long, sharp horns. She had read that the horns could grow almost as long as 5 feet. She shuddered at the thought of anyone wanting to harm such a beautiful creature.

The door burst open. In walked a well-dressed, efficient-looking man. He studied the girls. "I'm Brian Danbury. I'm in charge here."

"Thank goodness!" cried Bindi. "Can you please call our mums? We haven't done anything wrong."

"Is that so?" Brian towered over them looking unfriendly.

"We told your staff over and over again what happened. We're not making this up!"

Brian sneered. "And yet all the

evidence points to you two girls being up to no good. Until you come up with the names of your accomplices, you can spend a bit more time cooped up in here. How does that sound?"

"We've told you, we interrupted the men trying to break in. We're not with them!" said Bindi.

Brian stared her down, tapping a foot impatiently.

Bindi decided to change tack. She crossed her arms and adopted her most stern face. "This is totally unfair. When my mum finds out you've kept us here against our will, she'll be really mad."

Brian pulled a face in mock fear. "Ooh! Now you've got me scared. Police are on their way. You're not going anywhere."

And with that he left the room, closing the door firmly behind him.

The girls looked at each other as they heard the key turning in the lock. There was no doubt about it: they were being kept prisoner.

CHAPTER SEVEN

The sun was rising as Bindi gazed helplessly through the locked window. This was not what she had imagined her trek in Africa would be like!

The girls were stumped. They'd tried the windows and the door but both were locked. The phone on the desk was disconnected and, although Hannah had found her mobile phone in her jeans pocket, she couldn't get any reception.

Bindi began to pace. "It makes me so mad that those men are getting away while we're trapped in here!"

Hannah sighed glumly. "Why would anyone want to hurt such an incredible animal? And why are we getting blamed for trying to help catch them?"

Bindi didn't have an answer to either of Hannah's questions. Both girls turned as they heard the door being unlocked.

Hannah jumped to her feet. "About time."

A tall, thin, bearded man wearing rangers' overalls entered the room. He carried a tray of food and bottles of water that he set down on the desk. He gestured to the food. "Brian asked me to bring you some breakfast. Help yourselves."

The girls didn't need to be told twice. They were starving.

As she ate, Bindi tried to appeal to the man. "Listen, my friend and I need to get out of here."

He smirked. "Is that so?"

Bindi nodded. "We know some men tried to hunt the antelope last night and we have to stop them."

Suddenly the man was all ears. "How do you know that?"

Hannah piped up mid-mouthful. "Because we were there and we're being held prisoner here because we can't identify the men. We saw them cut a hole in the fence. They were up to something bad!"

The staff member shifted uncomfortably. "Maybe they had a different motive."

Bindi couldn't believe what she was hearing. "Why would you defend them? They were obviously doing something illegal."

As she ate, Hannah studied

the man more closely. He looked familiar to her. The more she looked at him, the more she knew she'd seen him before.

Hannah pointed to the man's face. "You've got something on your beard."

He rubbed at his beard self-consciously. As he did so a dark smudge appeared on his chin.

Bindi noticed the mark. "You've made it worse."

She took a step closer for a better look. "It looks like…face paint."

Hannah gasped. "I recognize you now. You were there last night. You're one of the men!"

Without a word the man strode swiftly toward the door and closed it. Then he turned back to face the girls. He looked very serious now. "You're absolutely right. I *was* one of the men breaking in last night."

CHAPTER EIGHT

Hannah and Bindi sat in stunned silence, staring at the employee-turned-intruder. They were both scared about what he might do to keep his secret from getting out. Should they scream for help?

The man took a deep breath before speaking. "Listen to me for a moment. I wasn't breaking in to steal or hurt an animal. I was trying to gather hard evidence to prove what's really going on here at this so-called 'sanctuary.'"

The girls gave him a quizzical look. "I don't know what you're talking about," Hannah said honestly.

"Let me explain. This is an animal sanctuary and breeding center, *by day*. It's a different story *at night*. They use part of the grounds as a reserve where men pay good money to hunt game for sport."

Now Bindi was confused. "No,

that can't be right. Thabu said it's for protecting the antelope."

The man shook his head and continued, "A colleague and I figured out what was going on here a few weeks ago. Antelope numbers were decreasing and we didn't know why. We've been trying to collect evidence ever since but it's difficult. Brian is a powerful man and security is really tight. We're searched whenever we arrive or leave the grounds."

Bindi shook her head slowly. "How do we know you're telling the truth?"

The man threw up his hands in frustration. He began to pace the room and seemed to forget about them altogether.

Hannah studied the man as he paced. "He could be telling the truth, Bindi," she ventured hesitantly.

Bindi shrugged. She didn't know what to believe.

The man paused and stared incredulously at Bindi. "Bindi? Steve's Bindi?"

Bindi looked at him tentatively. "Huh? Steve was my dad."

The man slowly sank into a chair. "This is incredible! Bindi Irwin."

Bindi looked over at Hannah, surprised. What was going on?

Suddenly, he was all action. "Are

you Bindi Irwin who lives at Australia Zoo? Daughter of Terri and Steve Irwin? Are you a global wildlife warrior whose mission it is to protect animals who can't protect themselves?"

"I am," admitted Bindi warily. "I'm just not sure if you are on the same mission."

The man thought about it. "I can tell you something that proves that I knew your dad pretty well. Okay?"

Bindi shrugged. "You can try."

"Your dad took a trip to Cape York three years ago to visit a croc sanctuary up there. Did he come home and talk about a guy called Mike Satchwell?"

"He showed me photos from that trip." Bindi stared at the man. It gradually dawned on her. "You're in those photos with my dad...but you didn't have a beard then."

Bindi made a quick decision. Turning to Hannah, she said, "We can trust Mike."

Mike stepped forward to shake their hands. "I should have introduced myself earlier."

"I guess your camera was the one they smashed?" said Hannah.

Mike let out a loud breath. "Did they? We weren't sure if they picked it up. We already had great footage of them hunting and we were going back to take a few more shots. I dropped the camera while running away. All our evidence is gone!"

Hannah smiled. "So you don't have a camera? But you do still have this." She searched in her pocket and pulled out a tiny memory card. "I saw it among the broken pieces of your camera when I bent down to tie my shoelace."

Mike's face lit up. "Fantastic. This is all the evidence we need! Smart thinking."

"Well, I'm not just a pretty face." Hannah couldn't help but feel pleased with herself. "And by the way, that lion that scared you off?"

Mike nodded.

"That lion was me."

Mike shook his head in disbelief. "You're kidding? We were scared off by a young girl?" He laughed. "Wait till the guys hear about that one. We'll never live it down."

Bindi cleared her throat. "Just a moment, guys. We have animals to rescue and a crook to expose!"

Mike began searching through the cupboards.

"There should be a camera in here somewhere. We keep one handy for the tourists. Help me look!"

The three of them started looking in every nook and cranny in the office. Finally Bindi let out a whoop of delight and held up a good quality camera, similar to the one the guard had smashed.

Mike took it and slid the memory card into the tiny compartment. "Fingers crossed that this will work."

The three watched anxiously as the card loaded.

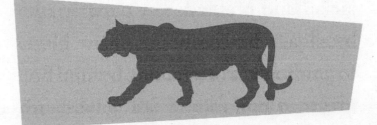

CHAPTER NINE

Bindi, Hannah, and Mike jumped apart a moment later as the door burst open. Brian stormed into the room, accompanied by two police-men. They were closely followed by Hannah and Bindi's mums.

Mike hid the camera beneath his jacket and pretended to clean up the breakfast trays.

"What's been going on?" Terri rushed over to Bindi and gave her a hug. "We got a call from the police saying you were being held here for questioning. We've just seen Thabu. He's outside with Robert and the horses. But he couldn't tell us what had happened."

Kirsten checked in with Hannah. "Are you okay, darling?"

Hannah smiled. "I'm fine, Mum."

Bindi was all business. "It's fine. We're fine. It's more like a case of mistaken identity."

Brian tried to take control of the situation. "You're lucky I haven't pressed charges."

Kirsten looked concerned. "I want to know what's going on."

Brian puffed up his chest. "And I want to know who these two girls are trying to protect. They damaged property of mine, they were trespassing, and we know they had help."

Terri bristled. She turned on Brian. "It sounds very much like you're accusing my eleven-year-old daughter of doing something illegal. You better watch what you say."

"And you should keep a closer eye on your brat. Creeping around in the middle of the night! This is a serious operation we're running here. It's no place for helpless little girls."

That last statement seemed to suck the air out of the room. Kirsten, Terri, Bindi, and Hannah all looked furious.

Bindi took a deep breath. "Mum, he's right."

"What do you mean?" questioned Terri.

Bindi turned to the police. "Look, I know I'm just a 'helpless little girl,' but I know this *is* a serious operation Brian's running."

Brian relaxed a little. "About time I was shown some respect."

"But it's not a sanctuary—in fact, it's the opposite of a breeding sanctuary. Big game hunters are paying money to hunt these beautiful creatures for sport." Bindi pointed to the poster on the wall. "And Mike here has proof!"

All eyes turned to Mike, who was hovering in the corner. He nodded his thanks to Bindi and spoke. "Bindi's telling the truth. A couple of colleagues and I have been collecting proof after hours." Mike looked Brian in the eye. "What you're doing is despicable."

Brian yelled at Mike, "This is outrageous! I refuse to stand here

and be accused of such nonsense."
He pointed to Mike. "Take this
man and these two brats away and
arrest them!"

"Calm down, Mr. Danbury, calm
down." The police placated Brian.
"These are very serious threats,
Mike."

"Of which we've yet to see any
proof!" said Brian, before receiving
another stern look from the police.

Hannah pointed to the bulge
under Mike's jacket. "I think the
pics on the camera might be the
proof you're looking for."

Brian watched with suspicion
as Mike pulled out the camera.

"But my guards said that camera was smashed…" He gulped as he realized what he'd just said. One of the police officers took a step toward him.

"Mr. Danbury—"

Brian backed away. "You can't possibly take a child's word over mine. I'm a very powerful man." Brian looked around the room, sizing up the situation. All eyes were on him.

Before anyone could do anything to stop him, he snatched the camera out of Mike's hand and took off out of the room.

CHAPTER TEN

Everything happened at once. The police radioed for backup. Brian made it out of the building and headed across the property toward the gates. Bindi and Hannah tried to follow on foot but he was too fast for them. Mike ran off to find other staff members to help.

Thabu was waiting outside with the three horses tethered nearby. Brian saw the horses and untied Pippi's reins from the fence before Thabu could stop him. He hastily mounted and tried to take off. But Pippi took offense at being treated so roughly. She pinned her ears back and gave a sharp buck. Brian managed to hold on and used the ends of the reins to let the horse know just who was boss. Pippi took off at a gallop in the direction of the gates.

"Thabu!" Hannah called out.

"There's no time to explain. You've got to stop that man!"

Thabu jumped on his horse and took off after Brian.

Robert was watching the chaos from the branches of a baobab tree by the entrance to the park. Just as Brian and Pippi cantered past the front gate, Robert let something drop from the tree.

From out of the corner of his eye, Brian noticed an enormous, hairy spider crawling on his shoulder. He let out a yelp and lost his balance. Pippi spooked and shied to one side. Brian went tumbling into the hard dusty dirt, landing heavily on his bottom.

A family of meerkats who had been watching the events broke into an animated series of barking and chattering. Here was the best entertainment they'd seen in ages!

Thabu caught up and jumped down to stand next to Brian, who was too winded to move.

The police car pulled up alongside them and the officers helped Brian to his feet, taking the camera from around his shoulders.

Within half an hour, the police had taken statements and arrested Brian, handcuffing him and driving him to the local police station.

Mike and the other staff gathered around Bindi and Hannah. Mike shook Bindi's hand vigorously. "It's not every day two young girls topple a dirty business and save the day. Thank you, Bindi. Thank you, Hannah."

"It's our pleasure, Mike," replied Bindi on both girls' behalf. "Us 'helpless' little girls can be quite useful sometimes!"

Mike laughed. He looked over at Robert, who was still up in the tree looking smug. "And I have to say, Bindi, your brother is one heck of a shot when it comes to the old spider drop!"

He gave them a parting smile, and moved over to Terri and Kirsten to explain the situation more fully.

Hannah and Bindi were now feeling seriously tired. They wandered slowly over to the baobab tree and Robert. They gazed up at the thick trunk and branches. Robert let out a mournful squeak.

"What's up, little buddy?"

"I can't get down!"

Bindi looked at Hannah with a wink. "We could help you if you promise not to give me any more eight-legged presents."

Robert stared down at his big sister and thought about the offer. "Actually, it's okay." He grinned mischievously. "Anyway, the view's great up here."

The tiredness retreated as Bindi remembered she'd been itching to climb a baobab tree from the moment she landed in South Africa. She looked over at Hannah. "If you can't beat 'em, you may as well join 'em."

As the two girls scrambled up the tree to join Robert, they were treated to an incredible view

complete with giant sable antelope
grazing contentedly in the park.

CHAPTER ELEVEN

A few weeks later, Bindi was checking her emails before bedtime and was excited to see she had one from Hannah. She'd been dying to know how things had turned out in Limpopo. She'd been worrying about Mike and what he would do now that his cover as a wildlife warrior was blown. She'd also been missing Kirsten, Thabu, and Hannah like crazy!

Bindi hurriedly clicked open the email.

Dear Bindi,

Sorry it's taken ages to write to you but SO much has happened since you left. We've all been really busy!

I can't tell you how much we're missing you and Terri and Robert! I'm so glad you've seen my home now.

Before I forget, Mike asked me to

let you know that he thinks you're amazing. Keep up the fight and keep being such a great wildlife warrior (even if you do have trouble with the not talking part! Ha ha).

So what happened after you guys took off? Well...

Brian was arrested for breaking the Prevention of Cruelty to Animals Act. His license to run any animal sanctuary has been canceled and he's facing charges. Mike now runs the antelope sanctuary. It has been restored to its original purpose, breeding the sable to protect and expand the species.

I was lucky enough to see a little

baby antelope born a few days ago. It was a long labor and the vets didn't think the baby would make it but she did. She's super cute and full of energy and already getting into trouble. We named her Bindi.

Much love,
Hannah

P.S. Thabu says that next time you visit, he'll take us out trekking and will make sure we don't nearly get arrested. He still can't get over the fact that he didn't hear us sneak out of the campsite.

Bindi turned off her computer. She'd have to reply to Hannah in the morning. Now it was bedtime.

As she lay in bed, she could hear the familiar sounds of the animals at Australia Zoo. Curlews were squawking and the dingoes were howling good night to one another. Africa had been a wild ride but it was really great to be home.

ANIMAL FACT FILE

THE SPRINGBOK

© Getty Images

- The springbok is a medium-sized brown and white gazelle that stands about 30 inches high.

- Springbok males weigh 73 to 106 pounds and the females weigh 58 to 93 pounds.

- They can reach running speeds of 50 to 56 miles per hour per hour.

- Springbok inhabit the dry inland areas of south and southwestern Africa. Their range extends from the northwestern part of South Africa through the Kalahari Desert into Namibia and Botswana.

- Springbok can be found in numbers of up to 250,000 in South Africa.

- Springbok "pronk" by leaping in the air repeatedly when they are nervous or excited. "Pronk" is Afrikaans for "showing off"!

ANIMAL FACT FILE

THE GIANT SABLE ANTELOPE

© Getty Images

- The giant sable antelope is a native species of Angola in West Africa. It plays an important role in Angolan society, where it is the basis of many local legends.

- It was thought to have been extinct until the species was rediscovered in 2002 at the end of the Angolan civil war, which had lasted for 27 years.

- It is a large, rare subspecies of sable antelope and is critically endangered. It is protected in natural parks, and hunting it is illegal.

- Giant sable antelope live in forests near water, where leaves and tree sprouts are always juicy and abundant.

- They are herbivores and feed on foliage, medium length grass, leaves, and herbs, particularly those that grow on termite mounds.

- Giant sable antelopes live in herds of 10 to 30 individuals, usually females and their young, headed by one male.

Become a
Wildlife Warrior!

Find out how at
www.wildlifewarriors.org.au

Become a friend of wildlife.
Make sure you report any
person you see mistreating
animals, especially our native
wildlife, to the police.

The adventures continue in

bindi
Wildlife Adventures

BOOK
3

BUSHFIRE!

"I spy…a blue-tongue lizard!" cried
Bindi, turning to her best friend,
Rosie, and holding up her palm.
"High-five, mate!"

The girls high-fived, giggling with
excitement.

"That makes the score seven to us
and six to Richard. We are so going
to win!" continued Bindi. The friends
turned triumphantly to Rosie's dad,

Richard, who was walking up the bush track behind them.

"There's an old saying, girls: don't count your chickens before they hatch," cautioned Richard. "In any case, unless you know the animal's scientific name, it doesn't count." He smiled, then strode past the girls, making his way farther up the mountain.

"That's not fair!" Bindi couldn't believe it. She had thought she and Rosie would finally beat Richard in a game of I Spy Wildlife.

"Dad, you're just trying to cheat because we're winning," said Rosie as she caught up to her father, with Bindi close behind.

"Two against one isn't fair either, but you don't see me accusing anyone of cheating." Richard looked at his daughter with a twinkle in his eye. "Nor do I think you *really* saw a rare spotted eagle about an hour ago. But as we have no video referee, I'll have to give you the benefit of the doubt."

Richard walked on, oblivious to the two friends exchanging glances and smiling. Was there anything Richard didn't know about animals? Some families played the regular game of I Spy but the Irwin and Bellamy families preferred their own animal-specific version. After all, they'd had lots of practice!

On this early morning, the

three keen walkers were hiking up Mount Ngungun in the Glass House Mountains near Australia Zoo. It was one of Bindi's favorite things to do. She loved being outside and seeing animals in the wild. Bindi also loved hanging out with Rosie and Richard. Rosie's dad was strong and athletic and always up for anything. He especially liked to win at games and never lost on purpose to save hurt feelings. No, he was ruthless in his animal spotting and it made Bindi and Rosie all the more determined to beat him!

Bindi raced on and soon overtook Richard. She figured that if she and Rosie reached the lookout before him, they might have more chance of spotting animals. His height definitely put him at an advantage for seeing birds.

"Wait for me!" called Rosie as she caught up with Bindi. The two girls puffed as they scrambled toward the lookout. "Come on, Dad!"

"Good things come to those who wait!" said Richard as he continued on leisurely.

It was already a very hot day and the last steep push to the top was hard going. Bindi could feel the sweat trickling down her arms, her legs, and the back of her neck. They couldn't have done the hike any later on a day like this. They would risk heat exhaustion and dehydration, not to mention having zero chance of seeing any animals—they'd all have sensibly found refuge in the shade.

The girls were out of breath and red-faced by the time they reached the lookout. They both took big swigs from their water bottles.

"Look!" Bindi pointed to the other peak in the distance. "Mount Tibrogargan looks just like King Kong!" The two friends marveled at the view of the majestic mountain peak to the east. They could see the sun coming up behind it, over the Pacific Ocean.

"Wow, it's really windy up here!" said Rosie, looking at the trees bending in the wind. It wasn't a refreshing breeze either, but a warm blustery one.

Bindi spun around, taking in the view of the surrounding bush and mountain peaks. Something to the west caught her eye. "Oh no!"

"What is it?" asked Rosie and turned to see where Bindi was looking.

Bindi silently pointed into the distance.

The stunning view was obscured by a thick haze of smoke. The friends stared at each other in dismay.

Richard finally approached the top. His face and neck were wet with sweat. "What a day! It's got to be over 80 degrees already and it's only 8 a.m." He mopped his face.

"Dad, we've got some bad news," said Rosie.

Richard laughed. "Don't tell me, you've just seen three more animals and won the game?" He chuckled. "I can take defeat gracefully."

Rosie pointed, and Richard turned to stare at the thick mass of smoke. Even as they watched, it grew darker and spread farther across the national park. The high temperatures and strong westerly winds were fanning the flames of a fire.

"Oh dear." Richard's expression was serious.

As head vet at the Australian

Wildlife Hospital, Richard was well aware that a fire in this kind of bush could mean hundreds of displaced and injured animals, to say nothing of threatening the homes and property of people who lived in the area.

He turned to the friends with a grim expression on his face. "We'd better hurry back, girls. It'll be all hands on deck at the wildlife hospital." Richard took one last look at the fire and turned to make his way down the path at a brisk pace.

Bindi and Rosie hurried after the vet. All thoughts of their earlier game had vanished. The sooner they got to the hospital the better!